A Small Texas Miracle

Jackie Smith, Ph.D.

To order additional copies of this book, contact:
Bookwhip
1-855-339-3589

Dedicated to Justin Kee,

Grandson, friend, adventurer, avid reader,

literary critic, brother, thinker, and philosopher.

It's been so much fun sharing our love of books!

Author's Notes

Dear Reader,

Texas is the home of cowboys, bull-riders, horses, cactus and mostly 100-degree weather, especially in the summer, but often year around. I got the idea for this book from reading about 5 Horrific Texas Winter Storms which went down in history and really did happen.

In 1957 what was called "The Panhandle Blizzard" went down in Texas history as one of the five worst, ever. This storm came in late March and dropped 10-20 inches of snow and even snow plows became stranded and couldn't clear the roads.

In 1985, "The Great San Antonio Snowstorm" came to visit Texas and was the worse winter snow storm San Antonio had seen in over 100 years.

In 1960, "The Houston Snowstorm" of 1960 came in February, 1960 and dropped over 4.4 inches of snow.

To illustrate how quickly the weather can change in Texas, imagine this documented swift change: In Bartlett, Texas in November, 1976, at 10:00 a.m., it was 72 degrees on the temperature gauges; yet just 2 miles to the north, in Temple, Texas it was below freezing.

Within one hour, it was below freezing in Bartlett as well. From 72 degrees F to below freezing in just one hour. Hard to believe, but true. The Robert Perry and Wally Herbert mentioned in this story were *real* explorers of the cold world of Alaska. Their exploits were exciting adventures.

In 2021 a week-long winter storm knocked out power for hundreds of Texas residents; many were without electricity and water for even weeks at a time. Those Texas citizens who had never seen snow in their lifetimes were faced with a storm most often seen in the northern United States.

This shows the unpredictability of Mother Nature.

Chapter One

HUNTER WAS TALL for his age, but very thin. Sometimes his Dad said he looked like all elbows and knees and his mother called him "Grasshopper". He lived on a little ranch outside of Austin, Texas. Hunter loved his ranch and he loved Texas; but every once in a while, he would read a book, see a movie, or watch a television special which featured places of snow, ice, and arctic temperatures and he would be swept by a strong desire to see these places. What must it feel like to walk amidst those giant ice glaciers, and feel those soft snowflakes hit your face and your tongue?

He read books of people who had moved to Alaska, both in early years and even currently, to make their fortune in that vast, cold, and quiet place. His Dad told him people could make a deal with the Alaskan government which would pay them to make their home and settle there if they would promise to live in Alaska eleven months out of each year. Hunter thought this sounded like a good deal but his father said, "Maybe so, but what if you signed a contract and then got up there and found out you made a bad choice?"

Hunter counted himself a true Texan, yet as many do, he still yearned for adventure in a totally different environment even if his father didn't agree.

What would it be like to strap on a pair of snowshoes? How fun would it be to wear a big parka with a fur lined hood? *Or even,* he thought, *a pair of those fur lined boots instead of his usual cowboy boots?* He had read many of the Jack London novels, his favorite being "Call of the Wild" and "White Fang". How exciting to ride standing on the back of a dog sled, racing other sleds and urging your team of dogs to run like the cold winter wind gusts across the snow and ice!

His friend, J.J., often told him, "You would like being there for about five minutes, buddy, before you'd be screaming to come home."

"No, I wouldn't. Just think what it was for those guys during the Yukon Gold Rush, J.J. Heading out for a country as big as Alaska to make it rich and facing that kind of temperature!"

"Well, yeah, but you're not Robert Perry or Wally Herbert, you're just a Texas cowboy. Me, if I had a choice, take me back to the days of the California gold rush."

"Well, you're not Santa Claus, either, but you sure pretend to believe in him! They both laughed.

"I'm not crazy! I want the gifts to come on coming!"

Every so often, the local weatherman on television would issue a statement something like, "Possibility, slim, but still a slight possibility of light snow tonight." Then Hunter and his friends would cross their fingers and say a little cold weather prayer, only to wake up in the morning and see the same old ground with not a sign of anything white. Or maybe a few little flakes here and there, but nothing to stick and certainly nothing to brag about.

He had never been on a sled in his life and he had even asked for one at Christmas this year only to be laughed at by J.J. and his parents. His father said, "What a waste of money that would be. Sled, indeed!" Sometimes he dreamed of waking to a huge snowfall, and school being cancelled. The dreams were so detailed and real that it was always a huge disappointment to wake to seventy-degree temperatures, even in January.

His parents had friends in New Mexico and they were always writing about the snow there, but the friends usually visited them in Texas during the summers, and he had never been to their home in Albuquerque or even his uncle's place in Montana.

His dreams were often filled with images of skiing down a snow run somewhere, hair blowing back, toasty warm in his big parka, wool cap, muffler wrapping his face and warm gloves holding his ski poles.

Now, it was Christmas break, and today he and J.J. were going to talk with their parents about possible future scholarships resulting from their rodeo memberships, and his parents supported the idea of a scholarship to A & M, where he and J.J. wanted to go someday. Hunter was an only child (something he regretted frequently) and while his parents would do all they could to see him obtain his goals, a scholarship would be a tremendous help. Here it was January, and a balmy, sunshine-filled day. He went downstairs to the kitchen, and found his mom fixing pancakes and his Dad drinking a final cup of coffee.

"Hey," he said as he sat down. What's up with you and J.J. today? Two whole weeks of no school, Christmas holiday coming up, you two must be feeling mighty cheerful." his Dad queried. "J.J.'s Dad is going to bring old Cherokee over here and leave him for the holidays so you guys can work them out each day. I told him that's okay, as long as you guys give them a good rub down after working them out, and make sure you put all your gear away each day. I know you are pretty good about taking care of Scorpian but I don't know if J.J. puts the same amount of care into Cherokee. Don't get lazy on me, you hear?"

His father usually never missed a chance to make fun of Hunter's choice of a name for his horse. "What kind of a name for a horse is Scorpian?" he would grin and ask but Hunter ignored him. He felt the name indicated a strong, fearless and somewhat scary horse. Which, of course, was not true. The horse loved Hunter and he would not have traded him for any other horse; even a race horse. Hunter always bragged that the horse could read his mind and could stop on a dime for him to jump off and hog-tie a calf in record time. He had many ribbons already to prove it.

"We won't Dad, I promise. Yeah, feels good to forget about homework and school for a while." Hunter said, "We're both going to enter the bulldogging at the rodeo at the state fair in February so we thought we'd practice some today."

"Well, take care with the calves you use and don't wear 'em out." His Dad was sort of grinning and Hunter couldn't tell if he was being serious or hinting that he and J.J. couldn't ever wear a calf out. As his father got his hat and walked towards the door he said, "J.J.'s Dad called and said you boys asked for permission to camp out tonight. I gave my permission but the weather forecast says a slight, very slight chance for snow this afternoon." He was laughing when he said it and Hunter laughed too and said, "Oh, yeah, maybe you should have gotten me that sled I wanted for Christmas."

His Dad was still grinning and he said, "You know what I say to the weatherman?"

"What?"

"Don't hold your breath, waiting for the first snowflake. Look at that sunshine out there."

Hunter left the sentence hanging and put away a huge stack of pancakes before he called J.J. and told him to have his Dad drop him over on his way to town and he and his Dad would give him a ride home later, if he didn't want to spend the night camping out.

He was kind of joking when he said this because he and J.J. never wanted to stay indoors when they could get outside. They loved camping out.

Even though he claimed he had already eaten, Hunter sat down with J.J. at the table and watched as he, too, put down a stack of pancakes. J.J. never was one to turn down food.

Any thoughts of his idea of a perfect January day in Texas bringing any snow were not in his mind that morning. When J.J.'s father dropped him off he had his sleeping bag. When he came inside, he told Hunter, "Our Dads' said we can camp out in the back yard tonight. That will be cool."

"Not as cool as the snow the weatherman predicted," Hunter.

Both boys laughed and J.J. said, "What part of 'a *slight* chance' did you not hear? I know it won't snow, but I know some new ghost stories to make the campfire interesting."

Hunter laughed and said, "You, ghost stories? Five minutes and you'll be hearing things. I'm okay with camping out, the tent is in the garage and so is my sleeping bag and other stuff."

"I couldn't find my canteen, but look what I've got here," He opened a sack and took out a bag of marshmallows and several Hershey Candy Bars and an unopened box of graham crackers.

"I haven't had smores in a long time. Good idea there, buddy."

The two of them made a pile of things for their campout that night and got Hunter's Dad's approval for their plans. Hunter's mother made J.J. call his mom and share all the plans.

They spent the late morning saddling up the horses and practicing their bulldogging skills. Then they cooled the horses down, brushed them good and put all the gear away before giving them some alfalfa and fresh water.

When they went back to the house to find some lunch, Hunter asked, "It does feel like it might be getting a little cooler, don't you think?"

"Um, maybe. I sure hope it does, even if it doesn't snow, a campfire isn't really fun unless it is a little colder than this."

After lunch they played a few video games in Hunter's room and checked their ice-chest for the campout by getting some bagged ice from the freezer in the garage for their perishables. They put in a new package of wieners, mustard, pickle relish, hot dog buns, their smores items, and a package of Oreo cookies.

"Well, we need enough to make sure we put the fire all the way out; ALL the way out."

"Okay, the gallon jug then."

Looking in the pantry, Hunter pulled out a package and said, "Look. I wonder if this will work as good on a camp fire as on the stove?"

"Popcorn! Sure, it will. Is it the kind that sort of fluffs up in a big foil ball when it's done?"

"Yeah, no need for a stove or a microwave."

"For sure, bring it."

Nothing extraordinary or unusual happened during the afternoon, and long before dusk the toys had their tent set up. Supplies moved inside and had prepared what would be their fire pit. They dug down several inches, and placed stones all around the perimeter, and lined it with gravel.

Then J.J. came up with an extraordinary and unexpected idea. "You know, this is kind of the sissy way to camp out, don't you, Hunter?"

"What do you mean?"

"Well, camping out in our back yard is what little kids do. We should move our campsite further into the woods."

"Do you realize how pissed my father would be if I did that?"

"Well, how's he going to find out? By the time he gets up tomorrow morning, we will be up and putting all this stuff away already. He will think we've been in this exact spot all night."

"Come on, don't be a chicken. Let's leave the tent here, and wait until we are sure they're in bed. Then we will move it on out to the woods behind the house here."

Hunter paused as if thinking it over. He wasn't used to disobeying his parents. Yet, he was ready to try something more exciting. "If we don't take the tent, what will we use for shelter?"

"Oh, boy, that's where the real challenge begins. We will build one. Just like I saw them do on that television show, "Naked and Afraid".

Hunter's eyes widened and he gazed at his friend in disbelief. "Your parents let you watch that show? They have naked people on there."

"Just their butt; not their fronts. My Dad watched it once and after that he let me watch it with him. He said it had some good survival skills on there."

"I'd like to watch it just to see the naked butts," J.J. said.

Hunter made a face at him, "Stupid. Naturally that would be your focus. The nudity. Not the survival skills. They have to stay like twenty-one days with very few tools and learn how to feed themselves and survive."

"So, from that show you know how to build a shelter?"

"Yeah, no big deal. But we can't do it with these little Boy Scout Pocket Knives. We will have to have something stronger."

"Like what?"

"Like the hatchet in my Dad's garage. Maybe even his machete."

"You told me once your Dad said not to touch that unless he was around because you could cut your arm or leg or something else off."

They laughed and Hunter said, "No, we'll be really, really careful. Sometimes they think we're still toddlers or something. Heck, we're half grown already."

J.J. said ruefully, I guess we are. I was eleven last month."

"Still, we'll be careful but it will really helpful cutting some branches for our shelter."

"Remember that kid at our school who was fooling with his Dad's gun and he accidently shot his little brother?"

"Yeah, that was horrible but his Dad should have had them locked up, like our Dads' do."

"Yeah, but my point is that we have got to be really careful. That's what its' all about. Being safe. Besides that, stupid kid was always getting in trouble. I'm just surprised he didn't try to being the gun to school."

"Let's go see what else is in the garage we could use."

"So, we're really going to do this?"

"Yeah, why not?"

"We have to get up early enough to break down the real camp and get back to the backyard fake camp."

"No problem. I never sleep long on a camp-over."

"Let's go on a recognizance mission and see whatever else we might need in the garage."

Rummaging through the garage, they confiscated an ax, a bow saw and a hammer and some long nails.

"Isn't that cheating?"

"What?"

"The hammer and nails. Those are not survival skills."

"What about camouflage paint for our faces since this is a recon mission?"

"Silly, it's not going to be really dark tonight, because it's scheduled to be a full moon. Who would even see the paint? It would be a waste."

"Well, okay, but it just sort of gets us in the mood, doesn't it?"

"I'm already in the mood, aren't you?"

"Well, yeah. Guess so."

"That reminds me, did we remember some matches?"

"Yeah, but I also have my little flint and tinder box. I think I can start a fire without the matches."

"Really?" J.J. looked admiringly at him. "I can't."

"Dad gave me the whole fire-starting kit for my last birthday."

"Lucky you."

"Now, here's the important thing."

"What?"

"We must stay awake until my Dad comes out here to check on us and the fire, and tells us good night."

"That's easy enough."

"That's like the signal he's going to bed and he won't be back until morning unless he hears us coming back in or making noise that something is wrong. And the only way I'm going back in is if you scare us both with those scary ghost stories of yours." He started laughing and after hesitating J.J. joined in on the laugh.

Sure enough, they had started a small fire and were roasting their wieners when his Dad stuck his head in and said, "Hi, guys. Everything alright out here?"

"Yeah, Dad. Perfect. Want a hot dog?"

His father laughed. "No thanks. You're missing some great tuna casserole and salad. Want me to bring you guys some?"

J.J. made a face and Hunter said, "I picked the right night to camp out. I hate tuna."

"Okay, sounds like you guys have everything under control. If you get cold or if you guys get scared, come on back in. Otherwise, I'll see you in the morning. Don't forget to bank that fire like I taught you, Hunter."

"I won't, Dad."

"That was easy, J.J. said.

"Yeah, but don't be too confident. Dad was a guy like us once. He is pretty smart."

"Yeah, but so are we," said J.J.; smarter than they give us credit for..."

They ate their hot-dogs, and like always, they tasted better than anything does when you cook and eat outdoors. Then they ate their roasted marshmallows, and topped it off with some Oreo cookies.

They kept a close watch on the house and after Hunter's parent's bedroom lights went out, they gave it an extra fifteen minutes and all was still and quiet. It was just beginning to get dusk.

"The most important thing of this entire adventure is that we keep very, very, quiet," Hunter said.

"Yeah," said J.J. "Everything depends on that. Absolute silence."

"First of all, prop the tent flap open with something, so we can move stuff out quietly. Go ahead and bank the fire so it's safe to leave the embers down in the pit."

"I think we should go and find a good spot in the woods first."

"Of course, you're right. Bring your flashlight, but don't turn it on yet."

The two of them moved out in the darkness, luckily it was a full moon and they could see fairly well even without the flashlights. They walked slowly through the underbrush, trying to avoid getting hung up on brush and every few minutes J.J. would say, "Is this far enough?"

"Sissy," Hunter would say and keep moving forward. Finally, after about thirty minutes, Hunter said, "I think this is far enough. How about you?"

"Yes," J.J. Answered, and Hunter perceived a little relief in his voice.

"Okay. Have you got the machete with you?"

"Yeah. I haven't really needed it, though."

Hunter didn't reply but secretly he was glad; he didn't really trust J.J. with such a tool. Sometimes he could be a little careless.

"I'm beginning to actually get into the explorer mode now; how about you?"

"Yeah, me too."

The built a three-sided lean-to with mostly old brush and small trees which were already downed by previous storms or even animals like the wild hogs so recently prevalent in Texas that ranchers were trying to get rid of because of all the destruction to crops they had been causing.

"Hey, what if we are sleeping really good and one of them hogs come crashing through?"

"Some of them have really big, curved tusks, but you know what?"

"What?"

"They have really good sense of smell. They will probably stay away from us. They are afraid of us, like we are of them."

"I hope you're right."

It took about an hour for them to transfer what they really thought were the bare necessities for the night. Then they built a safe new fire pit, and started a smaller, but satisfactory fire. This called for more roasted marshmallows, which turned into smores. Hunter allowed J.J. to tell a couple of his favorite ghost stories. He pretended to be a little scared but he had heard them all before, so if truth be told, he wasn't the least bit scared.

Finally, after they had each cleared a space for their own sleeping bags, they laid down a nice bed of pine needles from the trees and spread the bags to climb inside. Hunter remembered to carefully bank the fire as his father had taught him so they wouldn't really have a full fire by in the morning, but some live coals which could easily be restarted.

Once inside the bags, they talked about the upcoming rodeo, what they would like to do during this Christmas school break, and slowly, Hunter realized that J.J. was asleep, snoring lightly.

He grinned. He would make fun of his snoring in the morning. He felt his nose getting a little colder, and he pulled the sleeping bag up to cover it, and began to let sleep slowly overcome him. He felt warm and cozy in his sleeping bag and tried to imagine what the early discoverers may have thought, sleeping under the stars with just their horses for company and a blanket for warmth.

Chapter Two

THE NEXT THING that he was conscious of was that he could feel the cold, even though he was still aware of the sleeping bag. He blew out his breath and was surprised at the steam his warm breath made. Hunter glanced over at J.J. and saw that he was curled up in a little ball inside his own sleeping bag and Hunter acknowledged to himself that though it was daylight outside, he needed to get out of the suddenly insufficient warmth of the sleeping bag and stir the banked fire back to life.

As he tried to gather the courage to leave his warm, cozy little nest, he noticed a bright light coming through the sides of their shelter. It was more than just the morning sunshine; and was bright enough to almost make him close his eyes against it.

Hunter reluctantly rolled the sleeping bag down enough to pull his legs up so he could get out of the bag. As he did so he was suddenly aware of the quiet stillness all around their shelter. Why were the birds not raising an early morning ruckus? He remembered a long-ago story he had read which said, "The silence was deafening," and how he was impressed at the images these words brought forth in him. This silence was, indeed, deafening. There was an eerie hush and for a few seconds he felt afraid.

After he scuttled over to the fire pit where he had so carefully banked their late-night fire, he saw at once that there were not only not many coals smoldering beneath the black ashes; but *none*.

Sarcastically he said to himself, *oh, that shows what a good outdoorsman you are. Wonder what Dad would have thought about these skills? Oh, well, I best get some of the kindling we piled outside the shelter and start a new fire to warm up a little. I wish I had brought some breakfast fixins' like J.J. had suggested. Some bacon and scrambled eggs would have tasted really good right now. Also, the use of a camp stove, rather than the campfire would have been welcome. What had he been thinking?*

As Hunter moved towards had been the open side of the lean-to the open side of the shelter they had so carefully, but hastily constructed last night, he realized where all the light was coming from...Beyond where they had pulled brush to obscure the opening after they turned in for the night, peeking through was bright white which hurt his eyes and made him think of the lights in an operating room at the hospital.

I can't believe this! Hunter thought. Thinking he was still asleep and dreaming, he crawled towards the bright light and tentatively reached out a hand.

He was shocked to find out this was no dream. It was cold, *really* cold. And wet.

Snow? Really? Snow? He reached out both hands and realized it was indeed, snow and that it not only filled the open third side of the shelter, but there was a considerable pile inside the shelter as well.

No wonder I was getting colder, he thought.

He was beyond excited. He was ecstatic. Not only was there real snow, but they were, in effect, snowed in. Just as effectively as if a snowplow had shoveled it up against all the outer walls of the shelter, and inside the opening as well.

Without considering what the response would be, he scooped up a double handful and scooted over to J.J.'s sleeping bag. Pulling open the top, he thrust the snow inside.

The reaction should have been expected, but J.J. yelled a blood curdling holler, and trying to evade the cold, and to escape the wet snow, pushed Hunter down and almost climbed on him.

Hunter started laughing and said, "Guess what that it, buddy? Just guess."

J.J. Sat up and looked around. "What?" he asked, using his corner of the sleeping bag to dry his face off.

"Snow! Snow that's what it is. It showed last night. It's all around it. In fact, we are snowed in."

J.J. crawled over to where the entry was the night before, and started trying to use his hands to claw a tunnel.

When Hunter saw what he was doing he joined him.

Suddenly J.J. said, "Maybe we should try to get the fire going first, it will help melt the snow."

"That's going to be hard with no dry kindling," Hunter said.

"Well, you go through your stuff and find your fire starter kit or the matches and I will put my gloves on and dig a hole big enough to get the pile of kindling we stacked up last night. Probably the underneath part will still be dry enough to catch fire."

"What gloves? You have gloves *here* with you?"

"I always have my rodeo gloves just stuck in the side pocket of my backpack mostly because I don't lose them or can always find them easy. Of course, they are leather and no fur lining. But, hey, better than nothing, right?"

"I can't believe it!" Hunter said. "Once we dig our way out and get a fire going to warm up, we can see how deep it is."

"Heck, yeah. And we can have a snowball fight if there's enough snow."

"And a snowman, too. I knew I should have insisted on a sled. It must have been a premonition."

"Oh, yeah, I am so sure. It's probably the first time the dummy weatherman ever got a forecast right. They should give him a medal."

They were both occupied with their tasks and silent until J.J. sat back on his heels and looking at Hunter he said, "You're not going to believe this, old pal..."

Hunter looked around at him from his unsuccessful tasks of using his new fire-starter kit to try to get a fire going.

"What?" he asked.

"Every time I scoop a little snow out to try to make an escape tunnel, more falls down and fills it in. It just keeps coming."

"Well, that means one thing, any way..."

"What, except even with gloves my hands are freezing?"

"This isn't just a little snow. We really *are* snowed in. The entire lean-to is covered. There's no way to tell just how deep the drifts are out there."

"Still, the tunneling will work eventually."

"Yeah, we will keep hauling it out front the front, and then more will keep falling down to block our way out."

"Well, I wish you could get the fire started. That would help."

"How am I supposed to do that, with no dry kindling?"

"I'm really getting hungry, too."

"Wah, Wah, Wah. Don't be such a sissy."

Immediately Hunter was sorry he had said it. J.J.'s s expression made Hunter ashamed of himself. Usually, he was the one leading and with all the answers and here he was practically calling J.J., his best friend, a sissy. He needed to keep his cool so J.J. would, too.

He reached over and patted J.J. on the back as he said, "Ah, I didn't mean it, Pal. We're in this together. We'll figure it out."

Looking slightly appeased, J.J. said, "Do you think our folks have found our empty tent yet?"

"It's probably snowed under as well. Dad will be laughing because I finally got some snow, but he will drink his morning coffee and maybe even eat breakfast before he gets out a shovel or hoe or something to go out and dig a path to the tent and then uncover the flap to get inside. He probably thinks we are still asleep inside; cozy and warm."

"I guess camping out in the woods wasn't such a great idea, huh?"

"Well, let's be honest here, who would've thought?"

"Yeah, right. Stupid weatherman."

"Yeah, ever notice how they cover their butts? Like we might or might not get some snow tonight. Either way, they're covered, right? If it snows, they can say 'See, I told you so' and if it doesn't, well, they can say I said '*Maybe* or a *slight* chance."

"Yeah, and they had to go to college just to make guesses, right?"

They both laughed. After many tries, finally Hunter began getting some sparks and repeated efforts resulted in a tiny little fire on the kindling. Hunter scraped some of the unburned wood from the fire pit and when the fire began to take hold, smoke began to fill the space inside the lean-to. Both boys began coughing, but the snow where they had been tunneling *did* began to drip and melt.

Though their eyes began to run, they viewed this a small price to pay for the slowly melting snow at the door.

"If we could poke a hole in the ceiling, the let the smoke out, like the Eskimos do in their igloos, it would warm up in here and the smoke would escape."

"Hey, good idea! What can we use?"

"We could choose one of the branches of the shelter but we'd have to be careful not to take any of them that are helping support the lean-to walls or roof. If we're not careful, snow could drop down and smother our little fire as well as let in all the cold air."

When the two boys had chosen and then discarded several branches from their thick pine branches, they final picked one.

"One of us is going to have to climb on the back of the other one to gently pull our chosen branch out from the others, cutting some of it off, and leaving as much of the leafy part as we can. We only really want the stick, not all the branches."

J.J. nodded and replied, "Right. Well, you can do the climbing and cutting and pulling and climb up on my back piggy-back. I think I can hold your weight better than you holding mine. You're skinny and I'm much stronger and sturdier. I'll be able to hold you up there; but you better make it fast. I can't hold you up there forever with my eyes burning and tearing up."

Hunter didn't agree, of course, that J.J. was the stronger of the two, but he didn't argue with him. It was true that he was a chunkier build and was counting on playing football in high school one day. Hunter had already decided his only chance at sports would be running or basketball.

Having decided on their course of action, J.J. got down on his knees and hands, but the first try was a total disaster. Hunter got on his back, but before he even got his hands around J.J.'s neck or shoulders, J.J. dumped over frontwards, landing with his forehead and shoulders on the ground.

"Oh, that was great; just great!" Hunter said.

"Well, what did you expect?" said J.J. and then continued, "You didn't even let me get set for your weight or anything, I was totally off balance. Don't just leap on. Let me get set, then I will slowly stand with you on my back. Then, when you and are both stable, we will try it with your hands free."

The next time was a little bit better. J.J. actually got his hands around Hunter's legs, giving him somewhat a good hold before he attempted to stand up with the weight.

"Now, just hold on a minute before you move. It's kind of like last summer in the pool when I held you on my shoulders and we tried to unseat the other teams into the water. Remember?"

"Except," said Hunter, "There's no water, just ground and maybe soon, snow."

J.J. said, "Don't joke. Don't make me laugh. I can't do this is you make me laugh."

"Can you move slowly, very slowly, a little bit to your left? I see a good choice for a branch which we can get to and I don't think it whole roof will gave in without that one."

"I'll try but you stay still." He slowly began to inch sideways, but both boys felt very unstable and shaky.

In a couple of very tentative moves sideways, J.J. stopped and asked, "How's that?"

J.J. stood still and then he said, "I'm going to steady myself and you need to gradually free your arms and hands. No sudden movements; I mean it. Slow and easy does it, hear?"

"Yes, got it."

The first time Hunter reached out and barely touched the branch, there was a brief shifting of some of the branches and snow sifted down from a small opening made by the branch's adjustment to the movement.

"Hey," Hunter said, "The good news is that I don't think we will have to pull the whole branch out. Just that has made enough of an opening that the smoke is going out the front tunnel and this new hole as well. I can even see it going out."

"At least something is going right. Can we move back over so you can get off me? You're a lot heavier than you look."

"You have probably realized just like I have that all this was wasted effort..."

"How do you figure that?"

"With the fire now going, the heat was going straight up to the top and it's already melting some of the snow on the roof of the shelter without our help making a hole for the smoke."

"Oh, well, it was actually kind of fun," J.J. said, grinning.

"As I was saying there is good news…but also bad news."

Hunter felt his pulse go up a notch and he suddenly had to swallow. He tried to show a bravado he didn't really feel.

"On, yeah?" asked J.J., sitting on his sleeping bag and rubbing his knees and then shoulders. "And what's that?"

"It's still showing out there. Fresh snow. And it's very, very deep up against this lean-to and on top. I can't even guess how much is piled up already and who knows how much more will come? What if there gets so much snow the weight collapses it?"

J.J. was quiet for a few minutes and then he said, "Well, we'll deal with it, then. You don't know that's going to happen, right?"

Hunter wondered where J.J. was getting this new found confidence? Usually he always was the pessimist; he always saw the glass half empty and had to be talked into positive thinking.

"Well, you're right, of course and there's no use predicting the worst."

"But then, again, you have a point and we do need to have a back-up plan and be prepared for the worst, but expect the best."

Hunter again thought, *this doesn't sound like the J.J. I know.*

Completely jumping topics, J.J. said, "Do you think we can get some more wood to add to the kindling we have going now so we can maybe roast a couple of wieners. I'm starving."

"You ought to be more worried about how we're going to get out of here and home again instead of your belly."

"I think better when my stomach isn't growling." J.J. answered as he moved to the front corner of the lean-to where they had stacked some of the wood the night before. Though he had his gloves on, he could feel the wet, cold snow.

"Hey," J.J. said, "I wonder if the pond is frozen over? We could have fun sliding around even if we don't have a sled or any ice skates."

"Naw;" Hunter said. It would have to get below freezing and stay there several days for all that water to freeze. Wish it would, though. Hurry up with that wood, we're gonna' lose our fire here if we don't feed it."

"Then can we get the food out?"

"Sure. Gotta keep our strength up if we end up having to dig our way out."

As they prepared the wieners and put them on their wire holders to roast them Hunter said, "What if...what if we don't get out of here until our food runs out?"

"Are you crazy?" J.J. Replied, talking with his mouth full of hot dog. In his lap he had; as though protecting it, the package of the few remaining Oreo cookies. He continued, "Look how this snow is dripping and sizzling into the fire and down the walls. We'll be able to tunnel our way out if we have to."

"Yeah, but even if we tunnel, remember the ceiling of snow could be falling down all around us, getting us wetter and wetter. Besides, I don't even remember which direction we faced the open side of the shelter. Was it north...south? Or what?"

Wiping his mouth onto the sleeve of his jacket, J.J. replied, "Yeah, but have you forgotten my brand-new trusty compass? Let me find it in my backpack. I think it is in the bottom pocket. If I remember it right, we faced the opening towards home, and that would be south."

"We can't tunnel all the way to the house, you know. Especially on our hands and knees."

"Hey, remember that old movie with my man, Steve McQueen? The one where he rides a motorcycle and he is a prisoner of war? Remember their tunneling?"

"Sure, that was *The Great Escape*, but that was dirt falling in their faces all the time and can you imagine the weight of all that dirt?"

"True, ours is snow, but it is worse in some ways..."

"Name one," said Hunter.

"Well, stupid, it's freezing cold. For another, it's wet. And, have you forgotten it is *still* snowing? Wonder how many inches fell last night already?"

"Look who's calling who stupid. Whose idea was it to make it a *real* campout and move it from the back yard to the woods? Huh, yeah, I thought so."

"Let's not argue about that stuff now. We're here and I am not too worried. We will get out of here. I bet our parents already have a search party out for us.

"God, I sure hope not."

"Is that a prayer or what?"

"Well, I guess sorta; but I would like to think *they* think we are smart enough to find our way home. Give me some of those Oreos before you eat them all."

"Hunter, I'm not mad at you. Let's keep our cool here. I was just saying since we didn't tell your folks we weren't going to be in the tent, when they made it out there, what's the first thing they're gonna' think, huh? What?"

Hunter was quiet and then he said softly, "I know, I know. They're going to think we were kidnapped or something."

"Yeah. And my Dad is going to be so pissed at me. I'll be grounded for sure."

"Yeah, and they probably won't let us go to the rodeo and compete."

"So, what's our solution?" asked J.J.

"Well, here's the problems…We can't build up the fire because right now our rather unique igloo is our only means of shelter and if it melts and our surrounding areas are as deep as they seem to be, we can't just plow our way through chest deep snow all that way."

Hunter paused here and J.J. interjected, "You got that right. And even with the compass; which, by the way I still haven't found, we can't guarantee we will be facing the right direction, can we?"

"No, not really. We could be heading away from there, as far as that goes. Who knows?"

"Not that we have any experience with these conditions, but how heavy is snow when you are trying to push your way through it?"

"Geez, how would I know?"

"Well, you're the one who is so enthralled by snow and frozen ice places. Say, how's that old wish going now? Still want to live in Alaska?"

J.J. was grinning now and he added, "You're awfully quiet, old buddy."

When Hunter frowned at him J.J. made a face and said, "Don't get upset, pal, can't you see the humor in our situation? In fact, maybe you have the power of prayer and you prayed so hard you *brought* the snow. So, in theory, it's all your fault."

J.J. saw the beginnings of a grin on Hunter's face and he reached down and scooped up some of the mushy half-melted show from around himself and tossed it at Hunter.

They both exploded in laughter then, and Hunter said, "Well, maybe I had that coming, but you just wait until we get out of this mess. I'm going to wipe you out in our very first snowball war!"

Chapter Three

ONCE THEIR LAUGHTER subsided J.J. said, "Okay, "I'm all ears and have no original solutions on what to do. You be the leader; buddy and I'll follow."

"I don't feel like much of a leader right now, but I've been thinking..."

"Well, that's a start."

"Don't be a smartass, just listen."

"Sorry."

"Okay, first of all, I don't see any other way out of here, even if it is our only shelter; except to tunnel and find our way home. Our parents have no clue where we are and how likely is it, they will accidently stumble on us?"

J.J. nodded, without speaking.

"But near as I can figure, we were going about the tunneling all wrong. We were pulling the snow from up, overhead, then it fell on us, and we tried it again and the same thing happened. What if we deliberately tunneled from the lowest part. This would allow us to begin to make a passage out. We'd have to be careful in our tunneling. This is fresh snow, and it's not packed down. It's powdery and soft. We'd have to be mostly on our knees or scrunching down in a sort of hunched position. We'd have to go slow. We don't want to talk really loud or shout or anything which would make the snow fall so once we start, no talking unless it's an emergency. Got that?"

J.J. nodded quietly. His confidence was growing as it always did once Hunter took charge. He liked someone else being in charge.

It's so much easier to blame someone else if a mistake is made if you're not the one in charge. Let Hunter carry the responsibility. He was only too glad to hand the leadership role over to his friend. Besides, he thought, Hunter had always been the brains of their partnership.

J.J. spoke up, "And another thing, about the tunneling...have you forgotten there is no support on the ground, holding thew fallen snow up. If we tunnel from the bottom, it's just gonna' keep on falling until we have another hole to heaven."

"You know something, J.J.? You are absolutely right. So, toss that idea out. What next?"

Hunter resumed speaking, "Okay, now we don't want to get hypothermia unless we just can't avoid it."

"I that where your hands or toes freeze and you don't know they're frozen and they turn black and…"

"Yeah, and they sometimes have to amputate them; but that's not going to happen to us, friend. Do you bring extra clothing along? What's in your backpack?"

J.J. considered the question. "Well, considering that it was in the seventies when we started the day out yesterday, no. I only have these gloves in there because they're my rodeo gloves and they aren't all that warm. They're for roping and riding. No long-johns, unfortunately, but I did throw an extra pair of jeans in there and I have a long-sleeved shirt because I didn't want to get my arms really sunburned out in the corral. Extra underwear. Oh, and yeah, pajamas in case we didn't camp out. That's it, I think."

Hunter said, "Well, not too bad. In a minute we are going to strip down," he paused when he noticed the incredulous look JJ. gave him and he hurriedly continued, "Yes, just as quickly and efficiently as we can. Then you are going to put on the other pair of underwear, and over that your pajama pants, and your pajama top. Then, even though it's going to be difficult, you're going to put that other pair of jeans on over the ones you were wearing. I know it will be tough, but even if you can't zip them up, they will give you an extra layer. I wish we had something for your ears. That cowboy hat is not going to be much good, though we will wear it, especially when now and then we have a cave in or when we finally get where we might can stand up, and it is still snowing. Do you have extra socks?"

When J.J. nodded, Hunter said, "That's great! I am going to do this and so will you. Take the extra socks and use your knife to cut a hole in the heel, not too big; but then that part is going over your ear, and the toe to the top of your head. I'm hoping we can string the two socks through your hat string, and then retie it under your chin to make some protection for our ears. They will be especially vulnerable like our fingers and toes."

"The latest thing in frontier earmuffs," J.J. said.

"You got it. And on the top, first goes the pajama top, then the long-sleeved shirt, and finally your jean jacket."

"I wish we had one of those parkas' you always said you wanted," J.J. said.

"And a toboggan hat too, friend. So do I."

"You know what they say, buddy..." said J.J.

"What?"

"If horses were wishes, we'd all ride."

"Listen to you, the greatest sage since Shakespeare."

They began to take their clothes off, layer by layer, laying their removed clothing on their sleeping bags.

"Hey, this isn't going to work," said J.J. "The top of the bags is wet from the snow that dribbled through during the night. Out clothes will be wet."

"Not too badly if you hurry."

There was silence for a few minutes, while the boys dug through their back packs for other clothing. It worked fine for doubling the underwear, even with the pajamas, and the long-sleeved shirts. So did the pair of jeans they had spent the night in; but when they tried to put another pair over these, it was a "no-go". There simply wasn't room for another pair to go over the first. They admitted failure, and put the extra pair back in the back pack. When they got through with their make-shift ear muffs made from socks and looked up at each other, they broke out in laughter.

"I wish you could see yourself now," J.J. said.

"Well, you're no different. We should patent these and make a killing."

"Too bad they aren't wool socks."

"Who wears wool socks in Texas?" asked Hunter. "We are lucky we had extra ones with us.

When they put their boots on, and their gloves, Hunter looked at J.J. and said, "Ready?"

"As I'll ever be, I guess."

"When we first begin, we need to brush as much snow as we can in back of us or out as far to the sides as we can. Who goes first?"

Simultaneously, they looked at one another and pointed and said, "You!"

Then they laughed and Hunter said, "That's okay, I'll go first. Just remember to take it nice and easy. Don't go barging through there like a buffalo."

"Hey, I'm just as gentle as you are. Sometimes you act like the bull in the China shop, too."

"Whatever," said J.J.

They got down on their knees, Hunter in front, and slowly he pushed on the branches they had piled loosely in front of the opening the evening before. Immediately a bunch of snow fell down in front of Hunter. He said, "It's okay. I expected that. Here I go, pushing it back on both sides for you. Just continue to gently push it in back."

"Got it. On it," J.J. replied.

Hunter inched forward and this time just a slight trickle came down in front of him.

"Ah, better," he said.

He inched forward on his knees after using both hands like a scoop clearing some more snow out of the way to allow more access into their newly started tunnel. Hunter kept moving the snow back towards J.J. and he kept moving it back further inside the lean-to.

"It's not as cold as I thought it would be," said J.J. softly.

"Shhhhh," shushed Hunter, in a whisper.

Inch by inch they kept going on. Hunter noticed his jeans were wet at the knees now, as was the sleeves of his jacket. He also noticed his steamy breath out in front of him.

"How far are we going to try to go like this?" asked J.J.

"Dunno'," said Hunter. Then he softly continued, "Until the top caves in on us, I guess."

"Then what?" whispered J.J.

"Then we try to stand up. My knees and back are starting to ache from this crawling stuff."

"What if it's over our heads?"

"Then we raise our arms up and just try and push and bulldoze our way through."

"Can we stop for a minute or so I can turn my collar up? I have more snow going down my neck than in back on the path."

"Sure," Hunter said. Take a little breather but don't try and sit down; then your jeans will get wet all the way through and you'll really be miserable."

"I sure am hungry," J.J. said.

"Don't think about food. I would give my left arm for some hot chocolate."

"Wouldn't be a very good trade," chuckled J.J. "Then you could only dig on the right side."

"What time do you think it is?"

Hunter craned his neck and looked up at the snow. "Somewhere around lunchtime, I think. Hard to tell with all this bright white. I think I read somewhere being out in a snow-covered world can lead to something called snow blindness."

"Oh, that's great, buddy. Let's keep our spirits up. What other cheerful thoughts do you want to bring up?"

J.J. looked up and blew gently on the snow up around them. Immediately a hole began melting the snow there and it dripped down into his face.

"Hey, put some in your mouth. It actually tastes refreshing."

When Hunter looked at him skeptically, J.J. said, "Remember humans have to have water; even more than food."

Hunter reached out and scooped a handful and put it in his mouth. "My Aunt who lives way up north said they make snow ice cream every winter."

"Wonder what's in it?"

"She says sugar, vanilla, and snow."

"Hopefully she is careful where she gets the snow she uses."

"What do you mean? Oh, very funny, J.J. Like you mean yellow snow from doggie pee? How gross you can be sometimes."

"That reminds me...I need to pee," J.J. said.

"Not in here you don't."

"I mean it. I really, really have to go. What it I turn around and pee back from where we came?"

"How you going to get your pants open enough from your hands and knee position? And, if you are successful, how are you going to get all closed back up without snow getting all over you? Think about something else. Use your mind over matter. You can hold it awhile."

"I don't know...I guess I can try."

"Okay, let's move out. Enough resting."

They began inching forward again and J.J. might have been mistaken, but he thought Hunter had picked up the speed some.

Both boys had pretty much lost most of the warmth and heat they had brought with them when they left the lean-to and were acutely aware of how cold they were and how wet their jeans were. Especially on their knees. Their denim jackets had lost whatever effectiveness they once had against the constant snow. Hunter thought; but did not voice it to J.J., that the only good thing was that here in their tunnel they did not feel any wind. It was as though they were in some kind of cocoon and in a totally different world. He wondered if it was the same kind of feeling the astronauts might have way out in space sometimes.

After the stillness and isolation, they felt with only the faint noise of their breathing Hunter said, "How you holding up back there?"

"Good."

"Well, not me," Hunter said, mostly to make J.J. feel he wasn't the only one who might be getting discouraged. "I think I'm getting to feel like you and I are in some sort of solitary confinement."

"Well, isn't that the truth?"

"I guess so."

"I hate to break it to you, Hunter," said J.J., "but I can't hold it any longer. I am going to have to go pee. Either I try to turn around and go that-a-way or let you get far enough ahead you'll be safe."

"In which case, you would then have to crawl through the yellow snow. Do you think you could get off your hands, and carefully turn around on your knees to do it that way?"

"Like maneuver on my knees and turn around?"

"Exactly."

"Okay. You move on up a way, and I'll turn around on my knees."

After Hunter had gone several feet ahead, he said, "Okay, I think that is far enough. Go ahead."

Slowly, knee by knee, moving carefully, J.J. got turned around, and from the rustling sounds, Hunter figured he was arranging his clothing so he could finish his task.

Then, as J.J. said, "Eureka! What a relief that was!" There was a swooshing sound and the roof of the tunnel collapsed around them both. For a few seconds, Hunter could not even see J.J. There was so much snow blocking the two boys from each other. Hunter started trying to knock some off his head and shoulders and he looked up to see, very far up, a tiny round hole of gray/blue sky.

He heard a muffled voice coming from behind him. "Hunter, Hunter, are you alright?"

It sounded more like "Hunter, Hunter, Mar u tight?"

"Yeah, try to lean into the snow in front of you and push your way to me and I will try to dig towards you."

When he finally began to see J.J. the first thing he saw was the snow still piled on his shoulders and the top of his head.

"Hey, man, it's gonna' be okay. Knock some of that snow off. You're carrying more around on you than is out in front. Here, give me both your hands and I'll help pull up to me."

"Look, that should give you a boost," Hunter pointed up towards the hole showing the small view of the sky.

"Why is that going to give me a boost? It looks a long way up there."

"Yeah, but it doesn't look like it is snowing anymore."

"Maybe not but the sun isn't shining, either."

"I read somewhere that sometimes it gets too cold to snow. Maybe that's why it stopped. It's getting colder."

As J.J. was brushing off as much of the snow from his head and jacket he said, "Well, great and powerful leader, what next?"

Hunter laughed.

"What's so funny?"

"I just had a thought of how lucky you had all your clothes closed back up before the tunnel collapsed or something else might have been mighty cold, too."

"And that's your idea of humor?"

"Sure. We have to laugh at this adventure or cry and I'd rather laugh."

It was quiet for a minute and then Hunter looked over at J.J. and saw his eyes were beginning to water and turn red.

"Hey, hey, now, buddy. We're gonna' be fine."

"Aren't you even a little bit scared, Hunter?"

"Well, maybe just a tiny bit but we'd be crazy not to be."

"But what if we don't get home before it starts getting dark?"

"We'll build another fire and we'll write our own ghost stories."

J.J. grinned a little at this and said "Do we have what we need to start a new fire?"

Hunter patted his backpack rather forcibly and said with a strong show of bravado, "Sure we do. You don't think I'd leave my new tinder box kit back there in the lean-to, do you?"

"What do you say we try a new method for a while?"

"Like what?"

"Well, let's stand up like the men we are; off the hands and knees and even if it is just a little at a time, try taking turns in the lead and just plowing our way as far as we can each time."

"Hey, Hunter," asked J.J., "Think our families went to the sheriff or the state police and they have a B.O.L.O. out on us?"

"If they do think we have been kidnapped, sure."

"We'll be famous, my friend. Famous." Hunter was trying his best to cheer J.J. up as much as he could.

"I wish we had scarves or mufflers to cover our faces in this snowplow business."

"Me, too, but we don't. Do you think going backwards would help, we'd be putting backs into it?"

"I have never been good at doing anything backwards, I need to see where I'm going," said J.J

They paused just a few seconds and then both boys turned suddenly towards their left as an almost silent noise indicated someone or something's presence. Quietly, slowly, Hunter scooped several handfuls of show from that side of the snowbank and then he said, "Wow, J.J., come here. Look at that. Quiet now, don't move too quick or make any noise to scare him."

J.J. peeked through the hole Hunter had made and inhaled a deep breath, letting it out slowly.

Quietly, stately and majestic stood a beautiful stag. Although Hunter knew he must be aware of them, he stood completely relaxed, taking in his surroundings.

"He's at least a ten pointer," whispered Hunter.

"Yeah, where was he when Dad and me were hunting this year?"

Just then a small flurry of birds took off from the nearest tree and the deer bounded away zig-zagging as though to avoid their notice.

"Did you notice how high the snow was on him?"

"Yeah, but he still moves without any real effort. Can you imagine what it would be like to ride something like that instead of horses?"

"Like you were flying."

"Okay, move, it's my turn to be the cow-catcher."

"Hey, that's pretty good. Cow-catcher. Isn't that those pointed red guards from on the front of old-fashioned trains?"

"Yeah, it could plow through snow or brush or even help move logs off the rails. These modern trains are all streamlines and look like some kind of rockets. I liked the old coal or wood burners. My grandad worked twenty years on the Union Pacific Railroad and he had some really good stories to tell. Sometimes I think I was born in the wrong time."

"Do you really? I think that, too."

J.J. grunted and pushed more snow then he straightened up, took a big breath and repeated it.

"Hey, are your feet numb? I think mine might be. Is that frostbite?"

"No. Not yet, anyway."

"If we think they are getting that way, what should we do?"

"Well, in one of my Artic Explorer books it talks about a guy taking his socks and boots off and rubbing his feet all over until he got some more feeling back in them."

"Was he crazy?"

"I don't know how much was fiction or how much was true, but in the book it worked."

"If we decide we have to do that you're going first."

"Just think what a story we will have to tell our grandkids someday, J.J."

"Grandkids, heck, I just want to live to tell the kids at school."

"Goofy," only the good die young and you're not especially what I call good. At least not all the time."

"Thanks a lot. Now I know what our friendship is based on."

"You got to admit you and I are a long way from being perfect, kid."

"As our parents are so fond of telling us."

They laughed together.

"Remember when we went to scout camp one summer and they called our parents to drive all the way up there to pick us up because we had smuggled some beer in?"

"Do I remember? It seems like we were grounded forever and I even had my cell phone taken away."

"Yeah, that that girl in old Ms. Stevens class you liked so much said her parents told her to stay away from you. You were a bad influence. Remember that?"

Hunter said, "I don't remember it exactly like that."

"Naturally you wouldn't."

"We've had some good times, old buddy, haven't we?"

"And many more to come, don't get all maudlin on me."

"Do you think by now your Dad has noticed we took the ax?"

"No, he's sure to think we've been kidnapped."

"But why would kidnappers take the sleeping bags, the backpacks, the cooler and the food?"

"I don't know, but I'm sure they have all kinds of theories."

"You know, my parents have never threatened military school, but do you think this might be the time?"

"I don't know about yours, but my folks can't afford private school or a military academy."

"Well, Juvenile detention centers are free, if ordered by a judge."

J.J. halted in his snowplow pushing and said, "Really? They could do that for running away...and still on your parents own land?"

"Sure, they can do anything to teach a kid a lesson."

They pushed a little further and Hunter wondered how long he could keep distracting J.J. and keep his spirits. So far, J.J. is doing okay, but Hunter knew how J.J. was and he was not one to have a lot of determination. He was often too quick to give up if the going got a little tough. Kind of like on the Rodeo stuff.

He sure wanted to win, but practicing wasn't really in his equation on what it takes to win. He knew they were both cold and tired and hungry as well, but he also knew he could force himself to keep going. He wasn't that sure about J.J.

"Hey, Hunter," said J.J, "Tell me again how one day we will look back on this and think it's funny."

"We will."

"And tell me again how our friends are going to think we are heroes."

"They will."

"Can we scrape under the snow and try to get some really small kindling and see if we can clear a little circle here and start a little fire? Maybe we can melt some more from the top so we can at least see the sky a little bit again?"

"We can try, but I worry that if we are successful with getting one started, won't it just melt the snow above us and put the fire right back out?"

"Well, this isn't working; whatever it is we're doing; we've got to try something else."

Before Hunter could say anything else J.J. gave a squeal and said, "Oh, I cannot believe this, I cannot believe this."

"What?"

"Look," J.J. said, holding something out in his rodeo-gloved hand towards Hunter.

"Is that wheat I think it is?"

"Yes, it is! I kept feeling something in my jean jacket pocket; crackling and I felt up there, thinking it might be an old score card from school or rodeo club the last time I wore it, and it's an old energy bar."

"You've got to be kidding me! And you had it all this time?"

"Yep. Here, we'll break it in half and eat it."

"Not much, true, but right now it sounds like a genuine banquet. Hurry up, let's have it."

Sitting back on their haunches as much as possible, J.J. broke the bar into and handed half over to Hunter.

Complete silence for a few seconds as the two boys happily crunched on their own half, with J.J. happily making a soft humming sound from deep inside his chest.

"I will never make fun of your stashing food away all the time ever again. This is a life saver," said Hunter. "Check your other pockets."

"I did. This is the only one. My mom once found an old dried out sausage patty in my shirt pocket from when we went out for breakfast and I was full but refused to leave the patty behind. I had wrapped it in a napkin and was saving it for later."

Chapter Four

AFTER NON-STOP SCOOPING at the snow covering the front and top of the lean-to, J.J. was finally able to carefully reach out in the small tunnel and, feeling his way towards the base of the snow drift, and the "used to be" opening of the shelter, he gleefully held up a handful of kindling.

"Success!" he held up the scraps.

"Put them right here, where we had the fire banked last night. I think I have the tinder box set up. Be ready to get down here and gently blow if we get a spark to light the kindling."

Hunter built a small pyramid of the drier grass J.J. had handed him from his clutched hand The boys laughed together companionably and then Hunter sighed.

"Okay, back to the problem. Let's try your suggestion. First, though, let's deliberately poke and prod the top and try to get as much to fall down as we can, and then we push and scrape it over to each side to clear a circle to try for a fire. There will be fresh air coming in from above us, and we can't get any colder and wetter than we already are so we have nothing to lose."

J.J. took a hint from seeing Hunter pull his "sock-earmuffs" tight against his ears and did the same thing and after Hunter said, "One, two, three, go!" they attached the snow above them. Immediately there was a cold avalanche of snow which dropped down on them. They quickly began shoveling and pushing it off of themselves and to the side, and were thrilled they saw the small patch of blue sky above.

When they had pushed all but the wet, soggy ground aside into a drier feeling dirt circle, they stretched their arms under the piled snow on each side until they could feel some wet leaves and small brush and twigs. They brought small handfuls in, and Hunter got out his fire-starting kit. At first, he got nothing but sputtering and hissing sounds when the small blaze he got from the little twig and leaves he had dried on his jacket lining; but then, miraculously a tiny little flame dried and caught the leaf; then slowly, another and another.

Almost as they though they would jinx themselves if they got too excited with this small, but gratifying progress, neither spoke. They both attempted to dry the leaves they added to the little fire, gradually adding more sizes to the twigs. They did, indeed, get some rain-like melted snow from above, but gratefully, they noticed, more and more enlargement of the hold above so that the smoke was clearing through the hole, and the dripping moisture was further and further away from the boys themselves.

J.J. gave a gleeful shout, which actually started an avalanche of its own but rather than discourage them, they laughed and threw a couple of handfuls at each other. In the space of a few minutes, they were standing up, still surrounded by walls of snow, but definitely slushier and melting more rapidly as the warmth of the little fire expanded outwards.

Spontaneously they hugged each other. "We're getting out of here, 'Bro, going home."

J.J. grinned. "Not there yet, buddy.

"Remember, J.J," said Hunter, "This is probably just a big drift. As it snows, the snow falls down unevenly in different places, due to the wind and other things, it's not going to just cover the ground in a neat, even and flat covering—there will be hills of it and piles of it. The best thing for us is just to plow on through, straight ahead."

Which is exactly what they did. At first their enthusiasm carried them through quite a distance, and kept their energy level up but gradually, the cold and the now wet of their clothing began to raise their discomfort and dim their optimism and it became nothing more than a chore in persistence and determination. Neither wanted to cry "Uncle" yet and yet...yet, creeping back into their mindset was this sense of desperation.

Neither of them spoke of it to one another, afraid to be the one which admitted their fear of failure. It was probably this sense of desperation and the reluctance to admit even the possibility they would not get themselves out of this predicament which kept them going.

Suddenly dimly, as though from a long distance, they heard voices. Voices calling their names. They were almost afraid to believe it wasn't just their imagination; but as they pushed forward the voices got easier to decipher.

"Hunter," Yelled several voices together then would come a holler of "J.J." The two boys stood absolutely still, afraid to believe this luck.

Next there came the sounds of a snowplow in the distance and for a few seconds this noise drowned out the voices.

The boys gave out some shouts of their own, not realizing the sounds of the snowplow would probably drown them out. Then, suddenly, remarkably came silence and the snowplow stopped. The voices came back, and this time they were louder and Hunter and J.J. began to yell as loud as they could and there came responses, getting closer with every shout.

Finally, there was a break in the drift they were pushing through, and a bright red jacket appeared, followed quickly by a blue parka and several other people began screaming and yelling, some began to cry and the boys, wet snow and all, were enclosed by arms and hands, everyone trying to touch the boys as though to make sure these were real and not apparitions or visions.

Very quickly the boys were enfolded in blankets and riding in the back of an ambulance to the closest hospital.

The news of the boys' safe rescue passed like wildfire throughout the community. Flowers and card poured into the hospital room and as the boys were treated for what turned to be an extraordinarily light list of injuries, everyone felt they should fall to their knees in prayers of thankfulness.

Relief of the parents was so great as to make recriminations and even thoughts of punishments for the actions which had led to their close calls impossible. It was almost like when a child runs away from home, and turns out safe and sound it would be impossible to do more than hug them to their chest in relief at their being home once again safely. No punishments were meted out for the boys' initial misbehavior; everyone was too relieved they were home with no long-lasting harm. It was too difficult to even think of any "What if" considerations which might have arisen from their failure to follow the rules.

Epilogue

January came and went. February came and went. Suddenly it was in the eighty-degree weather again. Texas was back in the Texas weather once again and their snowy adventure seemed like just a dream.

They were announcing the winning scores for the calf-roping at the long-awaited annual rodeo, and while J.J. placed first in the calf-roping, Hunter took first in Breakaway Roping and Goat Tying.

Teasingly, J.J. said, "Too bad they don't have snowboarding or snow-man building. We are the only ones who would stand a chance in that. You ever wish to live in Alaska anymore?"

"Nope. I lost my taste for snow after our little adventure. I think I would like to visit the Sahara Desert instead." They both laughed at this.

First semester of school passed by quickly and it was the Christmas season. Wrapped presents began to appear under the tree and as usual, the two boys spent a lot of the time trying to guess what was in the gifts. There was one very big one in the corner, behind the tree at Hunter's house and try as he might, he could not guess what it might be.

"That is going to be the very first present I open," he vowed. "Can't you give me one little hint, Dad?" Hunter would beg his father.

His father stayed firm but did say, "Well, I will give you one hint. It is something you have asked for many times. Something you always wanted."

Hunter and J.J. both guessed and wondered and the days seem to pass very slowly.

Maybe it's' new western chaps, made to order especially for me...Or maybe it's a new hat...or a new belt buckle... Hunter would think of another possibility, and then discard it. Neither he or J.J. could agree on any guesses. The excitement mounted day by day and this was the first time Hunter could remember that he absolutely had no real clue to what was in the big box under the tree with his name on it.

Christmas morning arrived finally, and after Hunter's mother fixed herself and his father a cup of coffee, everyone began to open presents. As was their practice, his father would hand the gifts out one to one and they would be opened by the recipient and then, after everyone had seen what it was and exclaimed or examined it, another would be passed. Hunter was beside himself with excitement. His father kept handing out presents, but never the one in back of the tree until it was the very last present.

His father started to sit down and Hunter said, "Dad! Dad! There's one more present. Behind the tree. The big one."

"Oh, I almost forgot that one." He pulled the big gift from behind the tree and looked at the tag. Then he said, "I hope this one is for me. I love big packages."

"Oh, Dad," said Hunter. "You're just teasing. Look at the tag. You know it's got to be mine."

His father laughed and looking at the tag he said, "Oh, yeah. You're right. It says to Hunter from Santa."

Hunter stood and went to receive the huge package from his father.

He tore the wrapping off quickly and then his mother and father started laughing loudly, and Hunter gasped.

Inside the wrapping paper was a bright red, shiny, sled. Emblazed across in bright neon letters was the name: Airhead Rocket Snow Sled, for the avid winter sportsman.

The End

www.ingramcontent.com/pod-product-compliance
Lightning Source LLC
Chambersburg PA
CBHW020559130626
46552CB00007B/2959